WHEN THE WORLD IS DREAMING

WORDS BY
RITA GRAY

PICTURES BY
KENARD PAK

HOUGHTON MIFFLIN HARCOURT
Boston   New York

For Francesca —R.G.

In loving memory of Ruey-Yuh Hsyu —K.P.

Text copyright © 2016 by Rita Gray
Illustrations copyright © 2016 by Kenard Pak
Translation of Chiyo-ni's haiku by Jun Shepard

The text of this book is set in Bodoni Egyptian Pro.
The illustrations are watercolor and digital media.

Library of Congress
Cataloging-in-Publication
Data is on file.
ISBN 978-0-544-58262-0

Manufactured in China
SCP 10 9 8 7 6 5 4 3 2 1
4500595648

蝶々や
何を夢見て
羽つかひ

ah butterfly
of what do you dream
folding your wings?

—Chiyo-ni (1703–1775)

What does Little Snake dream
at the end of the day?
After the wriggling,
the sunning, the play.

Under a stone, curled up tight,
his shelter from the cool of night;
what does Little Snake dream?

Catching the wind, the kite sets sail;
and trailing behind, I am the tail!
Soaring above the tallest trees,
I dip and ripple in the breeze.

Sleep, Little Snake,
safe and warm.
Dream until the light of morn.

What does Little Deer dream
at the end of the day?
After the walking,
the grazing, the play.

In a bed of feathery ferns,
beside her twin, she gently turns.
What does Little Deer dream?

Rushing rain from a rumbling cloud,
the sky is flashing; the sky is loud!
But tucked beneath our mushroom cap,
we're safe from every thunderclap.

Sleep, Little Deer,
safe and warm.
Dream until the light of morn.

What does Little Newt
dream at the end of the day?
After the watching,
the crawling, the play.

In a bed of leaves and old tree bark,
cradled inside his pocket of dark.
What does Little Newt dream?

The squeak of rubber on rainy roots;
the ground is shaking from yellow boots!
But now I'm safe, so hidden from view;
my same orange self, but totally new!

Sleep, Little Newt,
safe and warm.
Dream until the light of morn.

What does Little Rabbit dream
at the end of the day?
After the hopping,
the nibbling, the play.

Beneath a shrub in a hidden nest,
head to toe with all the rest.
What does Little Rabbit dream?

Peas and carrots are tasty things,
but leaves of cabbage are perfect for wings.
Out of the field, and over a tree,
I lift to a cloud that looks like me!

Sleep, Little Rabbit,
safe and warm,
Dream until the light of morn.

What does Little Mouse dream
at the end of the day?
After the scampering,
the digging, the play.

Under a garden green and wide,
five soft tails curl side by side.
What does Little Mouse dream?

A shadow moving over ground,
slinking near without a sound.
With my tree bark boat and my pea pod oar,
I leave that cat behind on shore!

Sleep, Little Mouse,
safe and warm.
Dream until the light of morn.

What does Little Turtle dream
at the end of the day?
After the floating,
the basking, the play.

In a quiet pond, she stops her swim,
sinking to find an old tree limb.
What does Little Turtle dream?

Sky Turtle is playing hide-and-seek,
so I close my eyes before I peek.
Now she's here, right by my side,
and up I climb for a moonlit ride.

Sleep, Little Turtle,
safe and warm.
Dream until the light of morn.

What does Little Dreamer dream
at the end of the day?
After the running,
the laughing, the play.

In a cozy bed, all tucked in,
a blanket warm, up to her chin;
what does Little Dreamer dream?

My blanket is spread on the bedroom floor,
ready for the creatures to come through the door.
They gather around to see what I made,
and none of them feels the least bit afraid.

I have cabbage for Rabbit, and Mouse gets a pea.
These leaves are for Newt; they drifted from a tree.
For Turtle and Snake, some stones from the land,
and flowers for Deer to eat from my hand.

The moon sends down its silvery beams,
and we nestle together, in the best of all dreams.

Sleep, Little Dreamer,
safe and warm.
Dream until the light of morn.